JUAN BOBO

AND THE HORSE OF SEVEN COLORS

To Sam, for supporting my dream. To Jenna and Katie, for putting up
with a mom who writes more than she cooks. To Chuck Reasoner and
Bonnie Brook, for making life interesting. Thank you all.   —J.M.M.

Copyright © 1995 by Troll Communications L.L.C.

Published by Troll Associates, an imprint and registered trademark of
Troll Communications L.L.C.

Printed in the United States of America.

10   9   8   7   6   5   4   3   2   1

Library of Congress Cataloging-in-Publication Data

Mike, Jan M.
Juan Bobo and the horse of seven colors : a Puerto Rican legend /
retold by Jan Mike; illustrated by Charles Reasoner.
p.   cm.—(Legends of the world)
Summary: After winning seven wishes from a magical horse, the
foolish Juan Bobo wastes six of them on his way to try to make the
King's daughter laugh.
ISBN 0-8167-3745-2 (lib.)   ISBN 0-8167-3746-0 (pbk.)
1. Juan Bobo (Legendary character)—Legends.   [1. Juan
Bobo (Legendary character)—Legends.   2. Folklore—Puerto Rico.]
I. Reasoner, Charles, ill.   II. Title.   III. Series.
PZ8. 1.M595Ju   1995   398.2'097295'02—dc20   95-11765

JUAN BOBO
AND THE HORSE OF SEVEN COLORS

A PUERTO RICAN LEGEND

RETOLD BY JAN MIKE   ILLUSTRATED BY CHARLES REASONER

TROLL ASSOCIATES

O n the island of Puerto Rico there once lived a young shepherd by the name of Juan. Now, Juan was a perfect fool, a simpleton, and a dunce. He was known far and wide as Juan Bobo, because *bobo* means "fool" in Spanish.

King Luis, whose sheep Juan Bobo watched, was a very wealthy man. But his greatest pride was his beautiful wheat field.

One night a mysterious creature trampled down a portion of the king's wheat. The king was furious. He decreed that his wheat was to be watched every night. A schedule of guards was drawn up. But each night the result was the same. The guard set to watch the wheat fell asleep, and more of the field was trampled.

On the fourth night it was Juan Bobo's turn to guard the wheat. He left his house, carrying a long rope and a sack filled with bread and honey. He whistled as he walked for he wasn't very worried about guarding the king's wheat. After all, every other guard had fallen asleep and failed. He could scarcely do worse than that.

Juan Bobo set his sack next to a large anthill and sat down. "Since I can't have anyone visit me, these ants must do for company," he said as he laid out his dinner on his lap.

Now, bread and honey make a messy meal, even for the daintiest eater. And Juan Bobo was not a dainty eater. By the time Coquí, the frog, rang out his clear musical notes to signal the sunset, Juan was covered with honey. He stuffed the last bit of bread in his pocket just in case he woke during the night. Then he closed his eyes and rested his head against his empty dinner sack.

It was then that the ants decided to eat their meal.

"Ouch!" Juan Bobo slapped at a small ant that bit his leg.
"Ow!" He brushed two ants off his belly and one off his neck.

"Ow! Ow! Ow! Ow! Brother ants, leave me alone!" Juan Bobo pleaded. He slapped and brushed, but it did no good. Soon he was covered with hungry ants, nibbling at his honey-coated skin.

Juan threw himself to the ground and twisted like a madman. Finally the ants left.

nce more Juan Bobo lay down and closed his eyes. But the ant bites kept him awake. No sooner did one bite cease to itch then three more clamored for his attention.

Suddenly sweet music filled the air. Juan Bobo's eyes grew tired and heavy. He wished the bites would stop itching so he could sleep.

Juan squinted into the darkness. There, in the middle of the king's wheat field, a glorious horse tossed his head and snickered. The horse had a mane and tail of seven vibrant colors, from blue to indigo, yellow to red. They shifted like a rainbow in the night breeze.

Forgetting all about his ant bites, Juan stood and searched through his pockets. He drew out his last piece of bread and honey.

Looping his rope over his shoulder, Juan Bobo crept toward the horse. When he reached the middle of the field, he held out the bread and honey. The horse lowered his head and gently nibbled. Quickly Juan Bobo tossed his rope around the horse's neck.

To Juan Bobo's amazement, the horse spoke. "If you will set me free I will leave this field and never return. And to thank you, I will give you seven hairs from my coat."

Juan Bobo pulled his rope away.

"Each of these hairs will grant you one wish. But use them wisely, my friend." The horse seemed to smile as he spoke. Then he lifted his head and jumped into the air. In the few seconds it took for dawn to break over the mountains, the horse was gone.

Certain he had been dreaming, Juan Bobo looked down at his hand. Seven jewel-colored hairs were draped across his palm.

As daylight crept over the field, Juan Bobo left for home. When he arrived he tried to tell his brothers what had happened.

"You are such a bobo," his older brother jeered, before Juan could finish his story. "You should have captured the horse and brought him here. The king would have paid a great reward for a horse of seven colors. We could all be rich!"

Juan's younger brother smiled and shook his head.

"Let him be, *mi hermano*. He can't help it if he's a bobo. Besides, I am ready to leave."

"Where are you going?" Juan asked.

"Princess Aya has been very ill. The doctors say she will recover, but the princess barely eats and never laughs. King Luis has decreed that the person who can make the princess laugh will receive a great reward."

"*Bueno, mi hermanos!* Wait for me and I will help you."

"There's no time." His brothers walked out the door, waving good-bye.

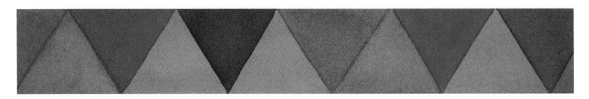

Juan scratched at his cheek, then his elbow, then his ear. He picked up the horse's hairs and sighed. He itched so badly he couldn't even think.

"I wish there was some medicine covering my bites that would stop them from itching," he said.

Now, everyone knows that the best medicine for ant bites is mud. In an instant Juan Bobo was covered, head to toe, with cold, slimy mud. He gasped and looked at his muddy hand. The red hair had disappeared.

He raised his hand to scratch his nose, then realized that his nose didn't itch! Now he could think.

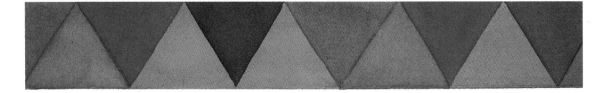

Juan walked out the door and into the bright sunshine. Before he could decide what to do next, his stomach began to grumble.

"I wish I had a sausage as large as my arm; one that never got smaller no matter how much I ate."

Before he could blink in surprise, Juan Bobo found that he was holding a thick sausage in his hand. This time the orange hair had disappeared.

Juan Bobo took a bite and began to walk. He walked and he ate, and the sausage grew no smaller.

"I know! I'll go to the castle and see how my brothers are doing. But I don't want to embarrass them," he said, looking down at himself.

Not only was he covered with mud, but his clothes were completely ruined after his night in the field. Dirty, stained, and torn, they weren't fit to dress a pig.

"I wish I was wearing a suit of clothes as fine as any that the king might wear," he said, slinging the sausage over his back.

No sooner was the last word out of his mouth than Juan found himself dressed in blue silk and red velvet. His huge feathered hat sparkled with gems, and his black boots shone like mirrors. He barely noticed that the yellow hair had disappeared.

"Oh, what a beautiful sight I am," he said. "But I'd hate to see these shiny boots get dirty. I'd better wish for a horse. A big black horse, fine as any in the king's stable."

Poof! A large black horse stood in front of him, and the green hair disappeared.

Juan Bobo jumped onto the horse's back and grabbed his mane. The black horse reared and pawed at the air. Then he raced off with Juan clinging like a burr to his back.

The horse bolted through a thicket of trees. Juan held tight as branches ripped his fine clothes and tore the jewels from his hat. Then the horse reared. Juan Bobo tumbled to the ground and the huge horse raced away.

"*Oya!*" Juan jumped to his feet. The air was filled with the buzzing of angry bees. The horse had dropped him right on a huge beehive! "I wish that there was something to keep these bees away from me," Juan said.

A flock of birds appeared in the air above Juan Bobo's head. There were red birds and blue, brown and gray. Some were large and some were small. Each time a bee threatened to sting Juan, one of the birds swooped through the air and snapped it in his beak.

"That horse was too big for me," Juan said. "I wish I had an old, fat donkey to ride."

"*Heeeaw!*" A donkey brayed in front of Juan. Now the blue and indigo hairs were both gone. There was only a violet hair left. Juan tucked it in his pocket and climbed on the donkey's back. He swatted the donkey on the rear, and the animal lumbered slowly down the road.

Ignoring the swarming bees and birds, Juan sighed and pulled out his sausage. It was going to take a long time to get to the castle on this old animal. He might as well eat and enjoy himself.

Toward the castle he went, nibbling his sausage. He passed through a small village called Gato, for it was filled with cats. One look at the flock of birds that flew about Juan Bobo's head, and the cats set up a howling and a yowling that was enough to make one deaf. Hissing and clawing, the cats followed Juan, each of them hoping to pounce on a fat bird.

Juan Bobo led the donkey through the next village, trailing bees, birds, and cats. This village was called Perro, for it was filled with dogs. Such a barking and a growling rose as had not been heard since when these dogs had chased after a swarm of cats.

And so it was that Juan Bobo finally reached the castle.

Princess Aya sat on her balcony with her ladies in waiting. All about the courtyard jugglers juggled and musicians played. But no one could draw even a smile from Princess Aya.

Juan Bobo, covered with mud and dressed in torn velvet, looked about as his fat donkey jogged to the middle of the courtyard. A crowd of angry bees buzzed around his head. Singing and whistling, colorful birds dove after the buzzing bees. Hissing and howling, a flurry of cats jumped after the birds. Yipping and baying, a bevy of dogs chased after the cats.

Juan sat up straight. With one mud-covered hand, he lifted the tattered hat off his head and bowed. Then he held out his sausage and smiled.

"*Buenos días*, my princess. Would you care for a bite to eat?"

**A**s her ladies watched in amazement, Princess Aya began to laugh. She laughed so long and loud that her mother and father ran out to see what she was laughing at.

"*Bueno!*" King Luis said when he saw Juan Bobo. "Will you live with us, *mi amigo,* so my little princess will never be sad again?"

And so it was agreed.

From that day forward, Juan Bobo lived in the castle with the king and queen and Princess Aya. He ate his fill of sausage, bread and honey, and other good things, until he was nearly as fat as his old donkey. And all he had to do in return was be a perfect bobo.

The horse of seven colors kept his word and never returned to the king's wheat field. As for the last magic hair, it is tucked under the soft mattress of Juan Bobo's bed. He has everything he could wish for and no use for it at all.

The Caribbean Islands

Puerto Rico

Although the tradition of the wise fool can be found in many lands, the stories of Juan Bobo, the folk hero of Puerto Rico, probably began with country folk. Juan Bobo stories were told by the *jibaros* to make fun of the often pompous and silly behavior of the aristocratic Spanish rulers and the Puerto Ricans who imitated them.

San Juan Bautista was the name given to the island in 1493 by the Spanish explorer Christopher Columbus. Puerto Rico was the name of the capital city, a name which means "rich harbor" in Spanish. Over the centuries, the names of the island and the city were switched. After its defeat in 1898 during the Spanish-American War, Spain surrendered control of Puerto Rico to the United States.

Puerto Rico is a tropical island with a pleasant climate and beautiful sandy beaches. The balmy weather is one of Puerto Rico's biggest attractions. Though the climate provides good conditions for growing tropical crops such as papayas and sea grapes, hurricanes may strike the island between the months of June and November. In parts of the island, rain falls nearly every day. Although much of the tropical forests that once covered the island are gone, many plant species remain, including the *flamboyan* with flaming red blossoms; giant ferns; and orchids.

Wild animals on the island include bats; mongooses; nonpoisonous snakes; and iguanas and other kinds of lizards. During the evening, a small frog called the *coquí* sounds its clear musical note. And the Puerto Rico Paso Fino Horse, which is famous for its delicate walk, is bred on the island.